¿Cómo crece? / How Does It Grow?

¿CÓMO CRECEN LAS ZANAHORIAS?
HOW DO CARROTS GROW?

Kathleen Connors
Traducido por / Translated by Diana Osorio

Please visit our website, www.garethstevens.com. For a free color catalog of all our high-quality books, call toll free 1-800-542-2595 or fax 1-877-542-2596.

Library of Congress Cataloging-in-Publication Data
Names: Connors, Kathleen, author.
Title: ¿Cómo crecen las zanahorias? / How Do Carrots Grow? / Kathleen Connors.
Description: New York : Gareth Stevens Publishing, [2022] | Series: ¿Cómo Crece? / How Does It Grow? | Includes index.
Identifiers: LCCN 2020011771 | ISBN 9781538269398 (library binding) | ISBN 9781538269404 (ebook)
Subjects: LCSH: Carrots–Juvenile literature.
Classification: LCC SB351.C3 C67 2022 | DDC 635/.13–dc23
LC record available at https://lccn.loc.gov/2020011771

First Edition

Published in 2022 by
Gareth Stevens Publishing
111 East 14th Street, Suite 349
New York, NY 10003

Copyright © 2022 Gareth Stevens Publishing

Translator: Diana Osorio
Editor, Spanish: Rossana Zúñiga
Editor, English: Kristen Nelson
Designer: Katelyn E. Reynolds

Photo credits: Cover, p. 1 Bill Sykes/Cultura/Getty Images; p. 5 Kevin Summers/ Photographer's Choice / Getty Images Plus; pp. 7, 24 (seeds) Heike Rau/Shutterstock.com; pp. 9, 24 (soil) Geography Photos/ Universal Images Group via Getty Images; p. 11 Stuart Fox/ Gallo Images / Getty Images Plus; p. 13 PhotoAlto/Laurence Mouton/ PhotoAlto Agency RF Collections/Getty Images; p. 15 Yuji Sakai/ DigitalVision/ Getty Images; p. 17 Victoria ArtWK/ iStock / Getty Images Plus; p. 19 emholk/E+/Getty Images; p. 21 sergio_kumer/ iStock / Getty Images Plus; p. 23 Mallivan/ iStock / Getty Images Plus.

All rights reserved. No part of this book may be reproduced in any form without permission in writing from the publisher, except by a reviewer.

Printed in the United States of America

Some of the images in this book illustrate individuals who are models. The depictions do not imply actual situations or events.

CPSIA compliance information: Batch #CSGS22: For further information contact Gareth Stevens, New York, New York at 1-800-542-2595.

Contenido

Zanahorias deliciosas. 4
Empieza desde la semilla 6
Vegetal de raíz 14
Tipos de zanahoria 20
Palabras que debes aprender 24
Índice 24

Contents

Yummy Carrots 4
Start from Seed 6
Root Veggie 14
Kinds of Carrots 20
Words to Know 24
Index. 24

Las zanahorias tienen un buen sabor.
¿Cómo crecen?

....

Carrots taste good.
How do they grow?

Crecen de las semillas.
¡Las semillas son pequeñas!

....

They grow from seeds.
The seeds are tiny!

Las semillas se siembran en la tierra.
Crecen bien en filas.

....

Seeds are planted in soil.
They grow well in rows.

Necesitan agua.
Necesitan la luz del sol.

....

They need water.
They need sunlight.

Las hojas salen de la tierra.

Leaves come out of the soil.

La zanahoria es la raíz.
Crece bajo tierra.

....

The carrot is the root.
It grows underground.

Las zanahorias empiezan
a crecer en la primavera.

....

Carrots start growing
in spring.

Las desenterramos
en el otoño.
Esta es la cosecha.

....

We dig them up in fall.
This is the harvest.

Pueden ser grandes
o pequeñas.

....

They may be big
or small.

Pueden ser naranjas.
¡Pueden ser amarillas!

....

They can be orange.
They can be yellow!

Palabras que debes aprender
Words to Know

semillas/
seeds

tierra/
soil

Índice / Index

agua / water, 10
cosecha / harvest, 18
raíz / root, 14
sunlight / luz del sol, 10